BARNES & NOBLE® READER'S COMPANION™

# The Lovely Bones

# Barnes & Noble® Reader's Companion™
Today's take on tomorrow's classics.

## FICTION
THE CORRECTIONS by Jonathan Franzen
I KNOW WHY THE CAGED BIRD SINGS by Maya Angelou
THE JOY LUCK CLUB by Amy Tan
THE LOVELY BONES by Alice Sebold
THE POISONWOOD BIBLE by Barbara Kingsolver
THE RED TENT by Anita Diamant
WE WERE THE MULVANEYS by Joyce Carol Oates
WHITE TEETH by Zadie Smith

## NONFICTION
THE ART OF WAR by Sun Tzu
A BRIEF HISTORY OF TIME by Stephen Hawking
GUNS, GERMS, AND STEEL by Jared Diamond
JOHN ADAMS by David McCullough

ALICE SEBOLD'S

# The Lovely Bones

BARNES
&NOBLE
B O O K S

EDITORIAL DIRECTOR Justin Kestler
EXECUTIVE EDITOR Ben Florman
DIRECTOR OF TECHNOLOGY Tammy Hepps

SERIES EDITOR John Crowther
MANAGING EDITOR Vincent Janoski

WRITER John Henriksen
EDITOR Matt Blanchard
DESIGN Dan O. Williams, Matt Daniels

This edition published by Spark Publishing

Spark Publishing
A Division of SparkNotes LLC
120 Fifth Avenue, 8th Floor
New York, NY 10011

ISBN 1-58663-866-1

Library of Congress Cataloging-in-Publication Data available upon request

Printed and bound in the United States

# Contents

# The Lovely Bones

# From Grief to Strength

*The Lovely Bones* is a moving, innovative tale of a family's tragedy and a girl's struggle to move on from earthly life.

○ ○ ○

**A SERIAL KILLER PREYS ON YOUNG GIRLS.** A gruesome rape and murder are committed in an underground bunker. The police never apprehend the murderer. This sketch of Alice Sebold's *The Lovely Bones* hardly describes the tender novel that has warmed the hearts of readers across America. Sebold transports us from the ghastly to the heavenly, from the sick to the pure, from the bloody to the transcendent with a grace that we rarely encounter in such tragic stories. Many readers, asked to summarize the plot of *The Lovely Bones* for interested friends, find themselves surprised by the unbelievable horrors of the novel's pivotal moment. Newcomers to Sebold's novel are skeptical that such a lurid true-crime spectacle could generate the uplifting feelings of compassion and forgiveness that so many readers describe.

But *The Lovely Bones* is much more than a graphic portrayal of bloodshed. Instead, the novel focuses on a crime's spiritual and emotional aftermath—consequences experienced on Earth and in heaven. George Harvey kills Susie Salmon, but the novel never treads in the realm of the slasher film. Sebold writes about the soul within the body, the spirit within the corpse—in the process almost dismissing the visual scene of mutilation that other authors and filmmakers would lavish with all their attention.

In only a few brief sentences, Susie tells us how her body parts are removed from the bunker, except for an elbow that a neighbor's dog discovers later. Susie sounds almost bored by her own dismemberment. Her dispassionate tone partly results from her being in heaven and having no more links with her earthly body. Susie's indifference to the physical aspect of her murder also serves Sebold's purpose as author. Sebold doesn't want us to be distracted by the gore and guts. She pushes us to transcend the physical and elevates us to the spiritual. Steering on Sebold's flight plan, we follow Susie's own path to heaven.

Susie's death becomes a universal symbol in *The Lovely Bones*, an emblem of all the horrors of human existence to which we must reconcile ourselves one way or another. Sebold wants to show us that evil and pain abound on Earth—but also that humans can overcome them. She emphasizes these two points with equal resolve. Susie never hits us over the head with spiritual lessons, but we nonetheless hear what sounds like a sermon running throughout the novel: Susie wants us to learn a lesson from what she says. She speaks to us directly—the last sentence in the novel is a direct command to us all—rendered in a manner more typical of a preacher than a fictional narrator. Susie doesn't just tell her story; she hopes to illuminate our own lives with it.

Sebold shows us wickedness not to shock us but to teach us something about evil. We feel the presence of evil every time Susie runs through the ghoulish litany of George Harvey's past and present outrages, every time we hear a detail about one of the girls raped and killed, and in every agonizing word of Susie's narration of her own murder. We focus on pain every time we watch Jack Salmon yearn for Susie's help in building his ships in bottles and every time we see how Abigail's and Lindsey's lives are derailed by Susie's violent death.

The grief of the novel's other characters is connected in Susie: the mother who makes a crude attempt at self-exploration, leading her to abandon her family; the sister who shuts down her emotional life; and the brother who loses all love for his mother. Their pain, in its various forms, derives indirectly from Susie's murder. Sebold frames the killing as a replay of Adam and Eve's first sin—the original dire act from which all later crimes and sorrows flow.

Yet *The Lovely Bones* teaches us how to acknowledge pain and evil while transforming it into something better. We understand why the murder scene is presented at the beginning of the novel rather than the end: Sebold wants it to be prelude to a whole family's moral and spiritual evolution, which she makes the true focus of her novel. Susie shows us the good that can spring from evil, if we wait patiently enough.

At the end of *The Lovely Bones*, when Susie finally uses the words of the novel's title, we discover that she doesn't mean her own physical bones, but the solid links between people that had grown after her demise. She speaks of "the connections—sometimes tenuous, sometimes made at great cost, but often magnificent—that happened after I was gone." Susie doesn't worry about her real, physical bones, ruined by evil. She's interested in metaphorical bones, the new spiritual connections that form after a loss: the new friendships, self-discoveries, loves, and marriages that blossom out of her tragedy.

# A MURDER MYSTERY TURNED INSIDE OUT

Sebold draws us into the intimate personal lives of her characters like a mystery writer. But *The Lovely Bones* isn't a mystery in a traditional sense. It presents us with no puzzle—the identity of the murderer is broadcast almost from the first page. We don't feel a pressing curiosity to uncover the culprit as we do in whodunits, since our narrator feels no curiosity. Already in heaven, Susie knows everything she needs to know—and reveals it all to us.

But like most mysteries, *The Lovely Bones* details the investigation of a murder and follows the traditional plot of a whodunit. We have a dead body in the opening pages, a detective on the scene, a killer on the loose and unrecognized by those around him, and a long wait to find out how it will all end. And like many murder mysteries we do feel a deep curiosity about the ending of *The Lovely Bones*. We may fight off an urge to flip to the last pages to see how it concludes. We may not need to see the murderer's identity unmasked, but we do want to find out whether he gets the punishment he deserves. We wait impatiently for justice to be served and the criminal to be caught, just as we do in whodunits.

And the murder-mystery feel of *The Lovely Bones* makes us interested in finding out as much as we can about the private lives of ordinary characters. The humdrum Salmon family would hardly invite our fascination if Susie weren't killed so gruesomely. We would probably yawn over a novel about exactly the same personalities, family dynamic, and marital dilemmas that lacked Susie's tragedy. Murder alone makes us sit up and take notice. We eagerly read through details that might have otherwise bored us: how Mr. Salmon makes ships in bottles, the books Mrs. Salmon reads, the number Lindsey wears on her soccer jersey. Just as in other murder mysteries, in which every minor detail can become an endlessly absorbing story if it somehow ties in with a killing, here too we willingly immerse ourselves in the daily details of an ordinary suburban American family in the early 1970s.

> Sebold joins two genres: the classic murder mystery and the psychological novel.

Sebold joins two genres: the classic murder mystery and the psychological novel chronicling family life and adolescence. She inverts the traditional whodunit to make the victim the narrator and lets Susie tell her story intimately in her own simple words, allowing for the introspective moments that are the flesh of psychological novels. Inevitably, this thoughtfulness renders *The Lovely Bones* more emotional and less objective. Sebold conveys feelings and yearnings as well as facts and information, avoiding the chilly, clinical style of most contemporary crime fiction.

The narration of *The Lovely Bones* reveals Sebold's strikingly original talents. Only a handful of writers have ever attempted such a reworking of the whodunit. The great murder mystery writer Agatha Christie once made the killer into the narrator—in *The Murder of Roger Ackroyd*. Masking his guilt behind a façade of impartiality, Christie's narrator suspends our suspicion of him until the end of the novel. The American novelist William Faulkner once made a corpse into the narrator—in *As I Lay Dying*—but Faulkner's narrator dies of natural causes, not murder. Sebold fashions a unique narrative of murder by making Susie central to the plot and emotionally forthcoming, while at the same time placing her at a safe distance from the events and allowing her to be omniscient.

Sebold's postmortem Susie adds the intriguing dimension of a narrator not simply dead but also in heaven. We don't often encounter this fictional device in modern literature—it's perhaps unknown since

Dante's medieval epic trilogy *The Divine Comedy*, the last part of which is set in heaven. As in Dante's work, Sebold's celestial storytelling casts a spiritual light on her story. Killed in innocence and honored by those who survive her, Susie becomes a Christ figure, as her name, Salmon, may suggest—early Christians used the image of a fish as a code name for their forbidden sect.

Susie's voice resounds from on high, as a stand-in for angels' voices or perhaps even for God's. A heavenly storyteller allows for a godlike perspective on earthly affairs, including crimes, and raises questions about divine vengeance and forgiveness. The vast majority of missing-children cases go unsolved forever, but Sebold lets us imagine that somehow, somewhere, someone remembers those children and punishes their offenders.

# THE END OF INNOCENCE

Murdered at age fourteen, Susie straddles childhood and adulthood. Up in heaven, wise to the ways of the world she only began to grasp when her earthly life ended, she mixes a childlike innocence with the street smarts of a grownup. She sums up her in-between status in the last lines of the novel, when she describes herself as forever stuck in a state of being "[n]ot quite" grown up. Sebold uses Susie's transitional age to explore the delicate balance between innocence and experience, one of the overarching themes of *The Lovely Bones*.

At times, it seems Susie has barely left her baby years behind. She wears a hat with bells in the pompoms when George Harvey lures her into his lair, and those little bells—which she tells us rang faintly in her mouth after her attacker silenced her with them—remind us of her tender young age. In heaven, Susie misses her dog, Holiday, almost as much as she misses the rest of her family, and her fondness for her pet emphasizes the girlish simplicity of her emotional connections.

Yet Susie, before her death, had started to enter adolescence and knew about sex. She cared about her looks. On the morning of her brother's brush with death, she applied Magenta Glitter nail polish to her toes—and her naming of the specific color points to the young women's magazines she flips through in heaven. We learn that on the fateful morning of her murder she changed outfits, throwing off her first choice of clothes to don the yellow bellbottoms that would be the last she would ever put on. While a quick change of clothes doesn't necessarily imply sexual maturity, Susie's concern with getting her look right hints that she has boys in mind. She dresses for the opposite sex—an adult habit. Susie's split-second kiss with Ray Singh also reminds us that she stands at the brink of sexual passage into adulthood. As Ray brushes his lips against Susie's beside her locker, she is surprised that this kiss happened, and the feeling of disbelief lingers even when she thinks back on it in heaven. Like any blossoming teenager, Susie's suddenly burgeoning romantic impulses catch her off guard. Ray's comparison of himself to Shakespeare's tragic character Othello—an ironically disastrous comment to make in a note given the day of her murder—betrays the frivolity of a first-time romancer. Ray and Susie aren't emotionally mature enough to be boyfriend and girlfriend. They both stand on the threshold of sex, but they haven't quite gotten there yet.

Susie's death at this transitional age means she'll forever remain aware of adult experiences but never taste them herself. From heaven, she'll watch the end of others' childhood innocence but will be trapped forever in the immaculate purity of a girl. Although she's raped moments before her death, Susie will always have the heart of a virgin, even if she has the mind of a teenager entering adulthood. Sebold prefaces the novel with a symbol of Susie's eternal purity—a snow globe that contains a solitary penguin in the snow, wearing a striped scarf. The tiny scarf reminds us of another wintertime accessory central to the novel, the hat George Harvey shoves into Susie's mouth during her rape. Sebold hints that the penguin resembles Susie herself, another lonely individual out in the cold weather alone, "trapped in a perfect world." Susie's perfect world, the heaven of her eternal innocence, imprisons her as much as it protects her.

## A GUILTY AFTERMATH FOR A FAMILY AND A NATION

The other characters in the novel—those who *aren't* trapped in Susie's state of innocent perfection—march into the guilt and responsibility of adulthood. Lindsey Salmon, although a year younger than Susie, strikes us as a more mature young woman from the beginning, as if she were somehow born more of a grownup than her older sister. We watch Lindsey read the French philosopher Camus while Susie reads a children's book. Lindsey doesn't share Susie's joy for playing with the family dog or eating candy. Lindsey's body seems to mature faster: Lindsey begins to shave her legs less than a year after Susie's death, but we never hear about Susie shaving her legs at the same age. Even her name lacks the childish ring of "Susie." (She had planned to start calling herself Suzanne soon, but she never got the chance.)

**After Susie's death, the entire Salmon family passes out of innocence into a new awareness of guilt, pain, and wrongdoing.**

Susie barely kisses Ray, but her sister thrusts forward boldly into the realm of sex. When Lindsey begins dating Samuel, the contrast with Ray and Susie's dalliance is stark. Susie's kiss in school resembles the daydream of a naïve 1950s teenager, while Lindsey's confident and self-assured fondling of Samuel's erection at camp belongs to the more permissive 1970s. Sex literally comes at the end of Susie's life, while for Lindsey it marks a beginning. She will grow into a sexually liberated modern woman, something her sister never had the chance to become. Susie, in heaven, remarks that while blood and horror coated the walls of her own "sex" (we may take this in the old-fashioned sense of "genitals" —another reminder of Susie's primness), her sister's walls were graced with windows. Sex gives Lindsey a new view of life through those windows, while it blinds Susie in many ways.

After Susie's death, the entire Salmon family passes out of innocence into a new awareness of guilt, pain, and wrongdoing. Before her death, the Salmons represent a stereotypically happy suburban family. The father works as an accountant, the mother as an old-fashioned home-maker, and the three healthy children grow up in suburban bliss. Even the name of their dog, Holiday, suggests the relaxed spirit of enjoyment that characterizes both the parents and children in the Salmon household. But after Susie's death, the happy home disintegrates. Mrs. Salmon cheats on her husband and then embarks on a voyage of self-discovery, taking up her earlier college interests again and finally abandoning the family altogether. Mr. Salmon submits to his own temptations too, feeling attraction for the sultry female neighbor who offers him delicious apple pie—replaying Adam's biblical discovery of sin in accepting an apple from Eve. After the fateful day in 1973, the older Salmons all step into sin, whether mild or serious, in their own way.

And America as a whole experiences the end of its own innocence at the same time as the events of *The Lovely Bones*. By 1973, the year of Susie's death, America had lost the naïve complacency that had sheltered it in the first years after World War II. The hippie movement that started in the late 1960s popularized the sexual freedom explored by Ray, Ruth, and many of the teenagers in *The Lovely Bones*—a freedom unthinkable a few decades earlier.

Abigail Salmon's search for self-fulfillment resembles the experiences of many women in the 1970s, as the feminist movement empowered women who were no longer content with domestic life—an abandonment of their traditional roles that many conservatives saw as immoral. The Vietnam War divided the U.S. population as no twentieth-century political issue had ever before, and questions raised by war protesters tested the conscience of a nation that had proclaimed itself the free and heroic protector of democracy worldwide. The Vietnam War made many Americans doubt their own innocence as a global power. Just as George Harvey snuffs out Susie's innocent life on Earth, the political and social climate of the 1970s did the same for the 1950s-style naïveté of the United States.

Yet *The Lovely Bones* doesn't ask us to weep for long-lost years of innocence, whether in our own childhoods or in our nation's youth. Sebold's novel as a whole isn't nostalgic or backward-looking, though she does look back fondly to the 1970s as Susie looks back to her happy girlhood. For the most part, *The Lovely Bones*, through Suzie's perspective, looks ahead. In heaven, Susie moves toward a final goal, the culmination (as we learn from her celestial den-mother, who explains all this to her) of her heavenly preoccupation with earthly affairs—the goal of letting go of those affairs.

In *The Lovely Bones*, we see that people in heaven can't fixate on their pasts forever. They do so for a while, until they've made their peace with those they left behind. Then they move on to loftier things we never glimpse and can't even imagine. By the end of the novel, Susie pays her dues to the living and settles her accounts with her family, and even with George Harvey. The living settle their score with Susie as well. Susie notes that Lindsey, with her newborn baby, can finally leave her sister where she belongs, in memories. Everyone moves on. They head toward the future, not the past.

Susie, like all of us, finally learns that peace and forgiveness belong to the future. The final pages of *The Lovely Bones* are imbued with a tranquility and harmony that we never sense at any point earlier in the novel, even in the contented days before the crime. We see a family meaningfully reunited after a long separation, a loss finally mourned completely and set aside, and a new home with a baby set up for Lindsey. The novel may have seemed dark, but it brings us to this bright and shining scene. All the trauma and horror of the murder scene leads us to this ultimate moment of happiness.

We may even need disasters to help us grow, as the Salmons need a disaster to change their lives. In the end, we may doubt whether the Salmons would emerge as happy individuals if Susie had survived. Abigail might never know whether she truly wants to be a wife and mother; Jack would never have known whether his wife cared for him enough to come back to his deathbed. Sebold makes Susie's final acceptance of her murder a symbol of how we all must deal with evil and grow from it. We can't bury our heads in the happy past, but must accept wrongdoing and tragedy and pain in our present life, grieve over them, and then let go of them.

## A sad coincidence

When *The Lovely Bones* was published in the summer of 2002, the novel's reviews shared newspaper space with stories devoted to the disappearance of fourteen-year-old Elizabeth Smart from Salt Lake City, Utah, on June 5, 2002. The blonde and winsome Elizabeth, who was last seen wearing red pajamas, conformed to many readers' mental image of the charming girl narrator of Sebold's novel. Just as in Susie's case, friends, family, and community rallied together to search for Elizabeth, gathering funds that promise a $250,000 reward for information on her disappearance.

# The Long and Winding Road

As they come to terms with her untimely death in different ways, Susie and her family take many paths to the same place.

○ ○ ○

## SUSIE SALMON

Susie dies in the opening scene of *The Lovely Bones*, but her voice resounds loudly on every page of the novel. Gone but not forgotten, driven away from Earth but not silenced, Susie draws the power in her voice not from her intelligence and talents—her sister, Lindsey, outshines her in these categories—but because she speaks to us from beyond the grave. Susie interests us precisely *because* she dies early on but her spirit survives to tell about it. She delivers a message of interest to all mortals in that she has information about the afterlife. She also has information about her previous life to share—details about her family, her friends, her dog. Susie straddles the border between our world and the next, an ambassador from the afterlife.

Susie's version of paradise—in Sebold's mythology, heaven conforms to our simplest vision of happiness—surprises us with its childish pleasures. Susie harbors no dark or complex desires, at least as far as we can tell from her description of heaven. She does not have sex in heaven, despite being titillated by Ray's kiss right before she dies. She goes to school, but only to chat with her friends, go to art class, and sit on the swings. In Susie's heaven, girls spin around and watch their dresses fly outward. They play with their dogs or place their feet on the tops of their grandfathers' shoes. This kindergarten heaven confirms that at heart Susie remains an innocent, pure child untainted by adult complexities.

Although we may tend to think of heaven as a static and unchanging place, the deceased Susie evolves considerably by the end of the novel. Initially, her heart remains tied by a thousand strings to her friends and family members. Susie's counselor, Franny, tells her that her aim must be to let go of earthly matters, but she can't—at least not yet. For most of the novel, Susie's attachment to Earth intensifies and shows no signs of abating. Her occasions for haunting her earthly family increase. Her love for Ray burns more brightly. Susie's involvement with earthly matters reaches its climax when she literally falls back to Earth. We think for a moment that heaven may not be Susie's permanent residence, that she may reverse the celestial order and come back to life.

But Susie's stay on Earth is short-lived. When she leaves for the last time, she finally says goodbye to her old dreams and her former connections. She finally feels fulfilled. She dreams of a sexual relationship with Ray and finally lives this dream—now she can live forever as a satisfied angel in heaven. Susie feels that her family has grown strong again and can take care of itself. She sees the "lovely bones," as she calls the connections that have solidified among her family members again and knows the Salmon family can now survive without her presence. At long last, their own lives have grown more meaningful to them than her death. When Susie sees Lindsey caring for her new baby, she knows that Lindsey has left Susie safely in her memories. Evolved now to a being more sublime than her former mortal self, Susie can move on to a higher level of heaven that we cannot yet glimpse.

## LINDSEY SALMON

Lindsey shares Susie's gifts but offers several more of her own. Blessed with the same irreverent spirit that Susie displayed in life, but with even more intelligence and charisma, Lindsey experiences everything Susie could have known in life had she survived. Lindsey impresses us as a superstar wonder child: she is blond and beautiful, she reads French philosophy for fun (she peruses Camus while Susie reads a children's book), she breezes her way through math and science classes, and she plays on the boys' soccer team—the only girl on the squad.

Even more important, Lindsey has a strong and independent character. She dares to break into George Harvey's house to search for clues about her sister's disappearance and narrowly misses being caught—and who knows what else—when Harvey returns home unexpectedly. Lindsey runs off with Harvey's blueprint for the underground bunker, affirming suspicions that he killed Susie. Her courage in taking these steps contrasts with her father's incessant nagging of

> At the beginning, we hardly know whether Lindsey misses Susie at all.

the police. Lindsey aims directly at what she wants, goes straight for the prize, and doesn't mess around with official procedures. She willingly becomes a criminal, breaking and entering, because the crime accomplishes her higher goal of justice. Lindsey follows a different set of rules.

Lindsey grieves in her own way, more brooding than weepy. Her reaction to the loss of her sister is less outwardly visible than that of anyone else in the Salmon family. Indeed, at the beginning, we hardly know whether Lindsey misses Susie at all. She says little about Susie or about what it feels like to have lost her. Lindsey tells Ruth that she never dreams of her sister; she dreams of rats chewing her hair. Yet Lindsey's silence doesn't imply indifference—far from it. We sense a yawning gulf in Lindsey's heart that words could not begin to express. In a similar way, her chilly relations with her family, as the rest of the Salmons struggle to support and console each other, aren't a sign that she wants to distance herself from them. The intensity of Lindsey's emotions make their expression difficult.

Lindsey's connections with her sister penetrate the fiber of her identity. She remains close to Susie in her thoughts and in her bones, even when she doesn't mourn her verbally. When Lindsey says that rather than dream of Susie, she dreams of rats chewing on her hair, we don't need to be professional psychologists to grasp what Lindsey is thinking. She identifies with Susie so closely that she dreams of being in Susie's place right now, interred and decaying somewhere in the earth. Lindsey doesn't need to talk about missing her sister because she nearly embodies her sister. Everyone shies away from Lindsey because she so stunningly reminds them of Susie—even Lindsey herself stops looking in mirrors, for fear of seeing Susie's image staring back at her. Lindsey reminds us, more than anyone else in the novel, that the loss of Susie afflicts everyone deeply, as if a part of their own identity has vanished.

## ABIGAIL SALMON

From the beginning of the novel, Abigail strikes us as a woman who has wandered into her role as wife and mother by mistake. She despises hearing her children call her "momma." Her eventual decision to leave her family, spurred by her fleeting romance with Detective Len Fenerman, comes as no great surprise. By this point in the novel, we've long felt a simmering dissatisfaction inside her, an urge to be elsewhere. Despite her old-fashioned New England name, which evokes duty and family devotion—think, for example, of Abigail Adams—Abigail has a strong independent streak. She must ride out her own storm and see where it carries her.

We sometimes detect a selfishness in Abigail. Of course, we forgive her because we understand that people in intense grief may do odd things. But in any case, the contrast between Jack's and Abigail's forms of grief reveals much about their different personalities. While Jack turns outward and deals with the social world, Abigail turns inward to herself. Jack gives—he gives constant advice to Len Fenerman and constant support to his children. Abigail takes—she hoards, for instance, the gift Jack's company sends for the whole family.

Susie hints that Abigail's self-centeredness goes back well before the date of her murder. She tells us that Abigail, during her pregnancy, gleefully ate all she wanted, rubbing her belly and thanking her baby for giving her license to pig out as she dribbled chocolate on her breasts. Although we can't condemn Abigail outright, we must acknowledge her tendency to view her children—even before she has any—as a way to satisfy and fulfill her own desires, rather than the other way around. She relies on her children as a false hope for contentment in life, a way to feel full and comfortable. She can't conceive of them as beings for whom she has to work, suffer, and make some sacrifices.

When Abigail loses a child, she loses one of her early false hopes and delusions—and thus finds a new life in loss in a way that her husband can't. While we never doubt that Abigail loved Susie deeply, we also feel that she never fully enjoyed being a mother to Susie or the other children —and Susie's death spurs Abigail to throw aside that role completely. Despite the steamy affair that occurs, it's not passion and sex that drive her into the arms of Detective Fenerman. Abigail is driven by a desire to explore her own identity. Sebold wryly sends Abigail to work at the Krusoe Winery—a place that evokes the name of Robinson Crusoe, the great fictional solitary island dweller who built a world for himself out of nothing. Abigail seeks solitude and introspection more than sex. When she completes her period of isolation, she can return to her family again, resuming her role as wife and mother in a more self-confident and self-aware way.

# JACK SALMON

Jack's Christlike nature makes him the saving grace of the Salmon household. Sebold reverses the stereotype of the mother as emotional heart of the family, making the father the emotional anchor and support for a suburban American family ravaged by tragedy. As sister and mother retreat into their own mental spaces after Susie's death, Jack's constant display of affection for Lindsey and Buck keeps the family operating emotionally.

In giving Jack the hobby of building ship models inside bottles, Sebold associates him with care, caution, and self-control—all the attributes required by such a painstaking craft. She also deftly hints that Jack encourages a love for adventure and exploration in his daughter Susie, who alone in the family respects his hobby and helps him with it. Ships carry people to see new lands, and Susie grows up with a healthy curiosity (though we sadly recall Susie saying that curiosity led her into George Harvey's bunker). Symbolically, Jack's shipbuilding hobby and his nurturing personality helped instill in Susie some of the values that made her a studious, careful, successful student and promised her an adventurous adulthood.

Despite Jack's obvious virtues as husband and father, he does have some failings. He strikes us as too passive in some ways, unable to act effectively even when he itches to take action. Jack knows before anyone else that George killed Susie, yet he manages to act on this knowledge only to the extent of telephoning the police department incessantly and nagging the detective, so much so that people start calling him a crackpot —thus actually lessening his chances of success. Lindsey shows what Jack *should* have done, displaying the active mindset her father lacks by daringly entering Harvey's house and coming back with hard evidence.

Jack also displays a violent temper. His judgment is hasty when he gets riled up. Again, his hobby of building ships-in-bottles implies a secret side of his personality. He keeps his feelings bottled up, and when finally uncorked they create havoc. When Jack wrongly suspects Susie's murderer of entering the field where she died, he runs after the interloper and nearly kills two innocent teenagers. A more decisive person like Lindsey would never do something so rash, largely because she would never have restrained herself from taking action like Jack.

## GEORGE HARVEY

Harvey embodies wickedness in *The Lovely Bones*. His gruesome killings of Susie and of many other girls and young women are crimes sprung from the unfeeling heart of a psychopath. Sebold never shrouds Harvey in glamorous mystery but uncloaks and unmasks him for us right from the beginning, shining the bright clinical light of a criminologist on his mind and behavior. His wanderings before and after his stay in the Salmons' Pennsylvania suburb remind us that his life extends far beyond the scope of Susie's murder. Yet her killing becomes a landmark for Harvey: after Lindsey secures evidence against him, he pulls up stakes and leaves behind his suburban lifestyle for good. Harvey's evil changes the Salmons forever, and the Salmons change his life just as much.

The thirty-six-year-old Harvey displays a gift many famous real-life serial killers have also possessed—he can maintain a normal outward appearance. Despite Harvey's bizarre project of building an African tribal wedding tent outside in December, and despite his proximity to a gruesome murder, the police let him go free after only a few questions. The investigators find him eccentric but not suspicious. Harvey doesn't lurk menacingly in the neighborhood or leer from his windows at neighborhood kids. He has a steady job, owns a house, and chats with neighbors cordially. On the outside he seems utterly normal. His hidden evil reminds us that wickedness may lie deep inside anyone.

As readers, we conduct our own detailed investigation of Harvey's personality. In tracing Harvey's obsession with houses, Sebold leads us into the darker reaches of his twisted mind and makes us speculate on the origins of his sickness. Harvey takes only the keystone charm from Susie's bracelet and leaves the others untouched. He builds beautiful, expensive dollhouses for wealthy clients who often wish to own a miniature replica of their own homes—suggesting that Harvey himself may wish to have a home just like the Salmons'. His actual house has the same floor plan as the Salmons' house, as Lindsey notes when she breaks into it. George Harvey may have been aspiring all his life—albeit in his sick, twisted way—to have a happy family and home just like the Salmons'. Unable to achieve it, he fixates compulsively on houses and kills girls to punish them for what the world hasn't given him.

Sebold allows us to diagnose Harvey even more accurately when she narrates part of his childhood for us. In the strange first few pages of Chapter Fifteen, the narrative flashes back to the 1940s, when George Harvey, a poor maltreated child, shoplifts with his mother and sleeps in cars. We sense that he learned early to view life as a theater of perpetual threats and constant danger. At one point, his mother wards off potential rapists by running them over with her car. Harvey trained himself from an early age in the art of avoidance and came to see crime as an everyday behavior.

Harvey also learns disrespect for the lives of women and children—in his opinion the weakest of the human species and the worst things to be—when he discovers how vulnerable he and his mother are. Later, when he kills women and children, we recall the scene of the attempted rape and find it to be a master plan for all his later horrors. Harvey affirms his own strength and identity by eliminating the strength and identity of young women. Ultimately, we see him as a vampire of sorts, living by killing others and by stealing their vitality, which he himself lacks.

## The mind of a murderer

Serial killers like George Harvey tend to be white, male, and heterosexual. Susie's murderer is thirty-six, but most serial killers are in their twenties. Much evidence exists to connect serial killings with childhood trauma—in *The Lovely Bones*, for instance, there are a number of flashbacks portraying the young murderer's tender but tormented relationship with his criminally insane mother many decades earlier. 56 percent of serial killers set fires as children, and 58 percent destroyed other people's property regularly. 71 percent isolated themselves from the company of others on a regular basis.

# RAY SINGH

The neighbor who would have become Susie's first boyfriend, Ray represents the ideal romantic male attributes that Susie doesn't live long enough to enjoy. He symbolizes Susie's thwarted teenage aspirations on a variety of levels. His dark good looks, like his mother's, make him sexually alluring to the maturing fourteen-year-old Susie. His intelligence and success in school make him even more attractive. His spirit of nonconformity is well matched with her own. His status as a somewhat isolated geek at school doesn't bother him any more than Susie's similar status bothers her.

In the small, largely white suburb in which the novel unfolds, Ray's ethnicity makes him a figure of exotic interest. While this exoticism may give him an advantage in romance, it also has the disadvantage of making him and his family outsiders of sorts, whom others in the community view as a bit suspicious. Sebold makes it plain that in the days after Susie's disappearance, the police's suspicions fall quickly and heavily on Ray because of his dark skin. Despite his innocence, absolutely proven by an airtight alibi, Ray continues to face suspicious stares from his peers at school. His classmates revile him, just as the neighbors revile George Harvey as rumors eventually spread, withdrawing the limited social popularity they had only recently begrudged to Ray.

When Susie returns to Earth for a few tantalizing hours, she comes for Ray. She returns not to see her sister again or hug her father—as much as she loves them—but to make love with Ray. As the resuscitated Susie, in Ruth's body, explores the mature Ray with his newly stubbly cheek and hairy chest, we see that sexual longing motivates her more than family ties or sentimental friendships. Sebold's refreshing honesty in showing Susie's passion for Ray affirms again that her novel is not nostalgic at all. It looks forward, not backward: the teenage girl in heaven looks not to her past family life but to her unrealized future of sexual maturity and love.

# Filling in the Blanks

*The Lovely Bones* means many things to many people—is it a portrait of loss, an inspirational text, a dark commentary on America, or all of these at the same time?

○  ○  ○

## Does Susie die happy?

**"YES, SHE DIES KNOWING THAT HER FAMILY LOVES HER AND THAT HER LIFE HAS BEEN SWEET AND MEANINGFUL. HER BLISS IN HEAVEN EXTENDS THE BLISS SHE ENJOYED ON EARTH."**

Susie dies in possession of the most important component of human happiness—the love of friends and family. Her mother and father remain married (a fact we shouldn't take for granted in the divorce-ridden 1970s), her sister and she share deep bonds of identity, she dotes on her little brother, and she adores her dog, Holiday. Susie's ties with all her family members are sincerely warm, unmarred by sibling rivalry, parental favoritism, or any of the other endless problems that can warp teenagers' relations with their families. Susie's love-saturated family life offers her many blessings, and her heavenly recollections of her former existence in the Salmon home make it plain that the affectionate and caring environment made her happy until the day of her death.

Susie also reminisces about her happy school experiences. Though some schoolmates find her nerdy, she doesn't experience the painful ostracism that proves a nightmare to some junior-high-school students. She fits in smoothly even with the crowd—Brian, Clarissa, and other hard-partying students—she doesn't wish to socialize with. Susie respects herself enough to maintain her dignity around them, and the members of the in-crowd respect her independence in return. Finally, she enjoys the glimmerings of romance in her friendship with Ray Singh. Because Ray kissed her before her death, she dies knowing that he desired her and perhaps (if she believes the note Ray sends her) even loved her. Susie attains—even if just barely before her death—the happiness of tender sexuality.

What's more, Susie enjoys a meaningful life as well as love. She has direction in her plans for the future. We have no doubt that had she survived, she would have used her industrious school habits to blaze a path to a successful career for herself, just as her sister Lindsey does later with her hours of studying to establish her therapy practice. Yet like Lindsey, Susie avoids being a workaholic drone. She shows such freewheeling spirit at heart that we doubt she would've turned into a nine-to-five workplace robot. Susie's favorite quotation, about writing against the lines on ruled paper, reminds us that she chafes at limits and rules. Blessed with a hardworking drive and the ability to enjoy herself, Susie seems prematurely wise at the young age of fourteen.

Susie looks back on a life without remorse or recriminations. She does have regrets (she bemoans the fact that she didn't have time to have sex with Ray, for example), but they're related to things she didn't yet have time to do—not on things already done. Susie has made no major slip-ups, committed no real regrettable errors, aside from the fatal error of following George Harvey. Of course, we can't say that Susie dies happily and willingly. No one—at least no satisfied and vibrant fourteen-year-old—would be happy to die. But by most traditional standards, we feel that she dies at a happy time in her life.

## "NO, SUSIE DIES UNFULFILLED AND THUS UNHAPPY. SHE MAY HAVE WARM MEMORIES, BUT SHE HASN'T LIVED ENOUGH TO BE ABLE TO CALL HER LIFE HAPPY IN A MEANINGFUL SENSE."

Human happiness requires more than a few pats on the head and a pet dog to play with. A truly meaningful sense of happiness demands more active involvement in life's experiences, undergoing and surviving life's tests. Susie doesn't live long enough to discover this, so her death at fourteen leaves her no more than a content but inexperienced baby. Her nurturing family environment and tender childhood friendships may have prepared her for a full and meaningful life to come, but they offer only that—a *preparation* for life, not a real life itself, rich in experience. Susie dies before she has a chance to live, so we can't consider her happy at death.

We can better understand the sad limitations of Susie's earthly existence by comparing her life to Lindsey's. Lindsey resembles Susie in so many important ways that, in Lindsey, we can almost see how Susie would've developed, had she survived. We see the contrast between Susie's furtive wishing and dreaming about sex and romance and Lin'nsdsey's actual, bold experimentation during her first encounter with Samuel. Whereas Susie's experience with sex stalls on the level of fantasy after her kiss with Ray, Lindsey's sexual development traces a broad arc from fondling to a full sexual relationship and eventually to motherhood by the end of the novel. Lindsey fulfills the erotic dreams and fantasies that heaven-bound Susie can only toy with in her mind. Aware of all she has missed, Susie can't be called satisfied in her celestial realm.

But Susie loses out on more than sex. She has no real opportunity to test her commitment despite doubt and hardship, as Lindsey must test her commitment to Samuel later by taking a deep breath and signing the deed on a ramshackle house he loves. Susie has no real chance to act courageously, as Lindsey does when she bravely sneaks into George Harvey's house and returns with evidence against him. Susie doesn't have the experience of exploding with irrational passion, as her father does when he goes half-mad with grief and frustration and nearly kills two innocent teenagers in a cornfield. Nor does Susie have the chance to experience the everyday challenge of keeping a grieving household up and running, as Grandma Lynn does. We witness a whole spectrum of passionate and complex human behavior in the Salmon household after Susie's death, all the while knowing that such experiences are forever denied to Susie herself, cut off well before her prime.

Sebold most directly shows us Susie's unhappiness in heaven by allowing Susie to *leave* it, if only for a short time. However exactly Susie's resurrection in Ruth's body comes about, we know that Susie perceives it to be a second chance at life—and we see how she yearns for a happiness on Earth that she doesn't know in heaven. People who die happy don't long for second chances, only the unfulfilled and unhappy do—and sadly, Susie is one of them.

○   ○   ○

## Why does Susie's death lead Abigail to commit adultery and abandon her family? Why does Sebold portray Abigail taking such an extreme action?

### "SEBOLD WANTS US TO SYMPATHIZE WITH ABIGAIL. SHE SHOWS US THAT PEOPLE SUFFERING EXTREME TRAUMA CAN BECOME SELF-DESTRUCTIVE AND RUIN THEIR OWN LIVES."

Despite her faults, Abigail comes across as a decent person. Sebold never portrays her as a monster or villain—she shows too much tenderness toward this well-meaning wife and mother to turn her into a caricature of evil. Although certainly far from perfect, Abigail nevertheless displays many admirable qualities in *The Lovely Bones*—reliability, sturdiness, and humor.

The wrongs Abigail commits derive from the tragedy at the heart of the novel. Susie's demise serves as a unifying reference point for the entire story, connecting all its events and character changes. Thus we have to see Abigail's adultery as deriving from the pain of losing her beloved first daughter. Before that fateful day in 1973, Abigail showed no signs of misbehavior, and we had no reason to see her as anything different from the average suburban housewife of the mid-1970s—perhaps a bit unfulfilled professionally but far from a home-wrecker willing to walk away from her family.

Sebold has Abigail behave in such a shocking manner because she wants us to see that Abigail has suffered precisely that: extreme shock. Trauma makes its victims behave in irrational, uncharacteristic ways. If Abigail had continued her motherly and wifely routine after losing Susie, Sebold would've had no way of showing us the disruption that Susie's loss has caused in her mother's psyche.

Abigail's choice of lover shows us how her traumatized mind works. Abigail commits adultery with none other than the detective investigating Susie's disappearance. We don't need to be psychologists to figure out that somewhere in her pain-distorted mind she connects her infidelity as a wife with her devastation as a mother. The mother who lost a daughter seduces the man who might locate that daughter. In the perverse mind of a person deranged by trauma, this leap seems logical. Sebold doesn't ask us to forgive Abigail on moral grounds—she asks that we understand what Abigail suffers and find a psychological explanation for her strange behavior.

## "SEBOLD WANTS US TO CONDEMN ABIGAIL FOR HER SELFISHNESS AND LACK OF CONCERN FOR HER HUSBAND AND CHILDREN."

While Sebold may not necessarily present Abigail as a villain, she still portrays Abigail's actions as morally wrong and wants us to condemn them. It's not easy to forgive a mother who flirts with the detective investigating her daughter's murder, goes in for a full-fledged affair with him, and finally decides to skip town on her family altogether. Abigail commits wrongs that go beyond mere life mistakes: they loom large in our minds—and in her family's—and they invite full and harsh judgment.

Sebold intends us to condemn Abigail, since her overarching message in *The Lovely Bones* concerns the evil, pain, and corruption on Earth that stand in sharp contrast to the pure goodness of heaven. In heaven, girls go to art class, chat on swings, and read *Seventeen* magazine. On Earth, girls are raped and slaughtered. That basic difference underlies the whole separation of earthly life from afterlife in Sebold's novel. Safely ensconced in the other world, Susie enjoys the luxury of morally perfect behavior, but on Earth, people stumble into bad behavior constantly. Life messily forces humans into compromising moral actions without their knowledge.

Among the Salmon family, Abigail is the most glaring example of the human tendency to behave badly, but others display the same tendency more subtly. Almost every member of the family does something wrong, something that either could or does hurt others. The normally upstanding and faultless Jack Salmon goes berserk one night and nearly beats to death two innocent teenagers in a cornfield. His rage transforms him temporarily into a monstrous killer. He may normally restrain this wicked side, but he definitely possesses a violent streak in a dark corner of his soul. Lindsey becomes cold and unemotional toward her family after Susie's death, withholding the support they desperately need. Buck treats his mother the same way later on, when she returns to see Jack on his deathbed.

Sebold makes Abigail part of an imperfect bunch—not just the Salmon family but human beings in general. Abigail's crimes are a far cry from those of the raving and murderous George Harvey in degree but not in essence. Both Abigail and Harvey have been hurt and both continue to hurt others. To varying extents, Sebold hints, we all do the same. We humans, at least as long as we reside on Earth, tend to evil—we can't help it. Sebold shows us the reasons for bad behavior in Abigail and the others but doesn't wish us to downplay their badness. On the contrary, she wants to show us that immoral actions and hurtful behavior represent the legacy of Adam and Eve, an inescapable part of life on Earth.

## "SEBOLD WANTS US TO SEE ABIGAIL'S WRONGDOING AS A PAINFUL BUT NECESSARY STEP IN HER SEARCH FOR SELF-KNOWLEDGE."

Sebold fails to condemn Abigail because she doesn't view condemnation as part of her job as a novelist. Sebold holds her mirror up to the world and shows us what it holds as truthfully as she can. She hasn't written sermons that tell us to avoid or follow a certain type of behavior—she's written a novel that allows us to make our own judgments privately. She avoids moralizing language and never either praises or condemns any character. Even the monstrous George Harvey receives some sympathetic sentences from Sebold's pen—portraying him as an abused child—that make it impossible for us to condemn him utterly.

Sebold shows us her characters' lives without judging them. Rather than pound the pulpit about Abigail's sins, Sebold objectively spreads Abigail's choices out for our examination, allowing us to see things from Abigail's perspective. Sebold shows us how Abigail's marital infidelity and family abandonment are steps that she needs to take on the path to self-understanding. We may or may not agree with Abigail's choices, but that doesn't matter. Given her goal of defining herself anew as an individual, stripped down of her role as suburban wife and mother, we see that her affair and her departure for California are the necessary first steps toward attaining that goal. Given that Abigail feels stifled as a wife in suburban Pennsylvania, it does make sense for her to leave the state. Given that Abigail questions her love for Jack, it makes sense that she would have a fling with another man. Our perspective here must be objective, not moralistic.

Just as Sebold objectively narrates the hurtful choices that Abigail makes, she objectively shows the pain those choices cause the rest of the Salmon family. She makes no attempt to downplay the anguish Jack feels or the utter devastation Buck feels—Buck's personality changes forever as a result. Yet again we must remind ourselves that Sebold's intent is to *portray* suffering, not to assign blame for that suffering. Like a landscape painter recording every tree in a forest, Sebold documents every bit of pain that results from Abigail's actions. But she always continues to treat Abigail's character with respect and even with admiration.

We may say that Abigail's so-called wrongdoings actually succeed in their goal of giving her life a new meaning—and that can only be beneficial to her family when she reunites with them years later. Sebold hints that Abigail's voyage of self-discovery may reveal aspects of herself that bring her closer to Lindsey, for instance. We see that Abigail reads home-decoration magazines before the tragedy, but we also know that in the old days she used to love French literature and dream of living in Paris. Abigail returns to this love during her rebellious period after Susie's death by reading the French writer Molière. Meanwhile, Lindsey reads the French philosopher Camus. Although Abigail makes mistakes, her newfound sense of self strengthens her bonds with her children.

# Are Jack and Abigail good parents?

## "NO. OF COURSE THE SALMONS ARE DECENT PEOPLE WHO LOVE THEIR KIDS. BUT AS PARENTS THEY SHOW MANY FAILINGS."

Although Sebold introduces us to Jack and Abigail Salmon with sympathy and understanding, she doesn't shy away from showing us their defects as mother and father to their three children. We see the sensitive sides of both of them, but that sensitivity often gets the better of them and makes them questionable adult role models for their kids. We may admire and love Jack and Abigail as individuals, for their humanity and emotional depth, but we can't really admire them as parents.

Jack displays integrity and personal virtues. His devotion to his wife remains unshaken after her long absence—an abandonment many husbands wouldn't forgive. His grief over Susie surpasses that of anyone else in the family in its range and depth. And his painstaking attention in building model ships in bottles reveals the same extraordinary patience and care that he takes in helping his family navigate through their grief after Susie's demise.

But likable characters don't always make good parents. Jack's personal virtues, as much as we like them, nevertheless also make him a poor paternal role model for his children. The incredible patience he displays at home after Susie's death warps into a paralyzing passivity. Jack suspects George Harvey long before anyone else does but can't bring himself to act on his suspicions. He calls the police constantly and whines to them ineffectually. We see Lindsey yearning for her father to take active measures and prove his paternal love with bold actions, since she ends up doing what he should have done—sneaking into Harvey's house—and reporting to him about it. Lindsey ultimately must step in to perform her father's duties herself. When Jack finally does take active steps in pursuing Susie's killer, he bungles it horribly, pursuing the wrong party. We see Jack as a nice guy but not at all a hero, especially at a moment when his family desperately needs their father to be heroic.

Abigail, in the same way, does possess admirable qualities, but in the end we can't nominate her for Mother of the Year. She displays an earnest need to explore her inner self, to find out her true identity, and we can't help but marvel at the sheer guts of a woman who could sacrifice her beloved family and home in order to pursue that aim of self-knowledge. Abigail strikes us as a philosophical wonderer who somehow wound up as a housewife in suburban Pennsylvania. In leaving, she dares to discover her true calling against all odds.

But Abigail, like her husband, displays individual virtues that don't necessarily make her a good parent. We may praise a twenty-year-old single woman for her need to explore her inner self and work in solitude in a California winery, but we can't praise a mother in her thirties who leaves her young children and devoted husband to do so. Abigail should've tried to find a way to discover her true self while remaining at home with her children. She could've read French literature at home in Pennsylvania and even bonded with Lindsey (who also reads French writers) in the process. But Abigail selfishly ignores that option and leaves town instead.

By the end of *The Lovely Bones*, we may have come to respect both Jack and Abigail as people. We may even admire what they've accomplished in their personal lives. But none of us would dream of enrolling either of them in a Parent of the Year contest.

## "YES, THE SALMONS ARE GOOD PARENTS. THEY DISPLAY MANY GOOD QUALITIES—SOMETIMES NOT OBVIOUS AT FIRST SIGHT—THAT MAKE THEM WELL-SUITED TO RAISING THEIR CHILDREN."

Jack and Abigail excel as parents. While they screw up now and then, and while Abigail even needs a few years of time off to regain her bearings, we have to remember that they've both been through the unimaginable trauma of losing their firstborn child. Their minor errors of judgment only show more clearly their character and the sensitivity of their souls—the complex personalities that make them good people and good parents. Abigail never cheated on Jack before Susie's death, which leads us to believe that she only strays later as a result of her grief. And Jack never showed any tendencies toward whiny passivity before his daughter's murder. He shows not an abiding character flaw but only the temporary damage that results from the unthinkable loss he's suffered.

Jack may err in becoming depressed and passive, moping around at home too much after Susie's death. And he certainly displays bad judgment in going after the two teenagers in the cornfield, surrendering to a murderous rage for a moment. But both these failings derive from an admirable trait—an excess of concern for his family and his lost daughter. Jack occasionally overreacts to the situation, but we can't say his love for Susie fails or that he shows anything less than the highest commitment to his family. When Jack runs amok in the cornfield chasing the person he imagines to be Susie's killer, he resembles King Lear raging on the moors. He only affirms his fatherly merits in doing so, since like Lear he's gone mad from love for his daughters.

Most of us probably find it harder to forgive Abigail, but she too shows strength of character in following her dreams—a strength that makes her a better mother than she would have been otherwise. Yes, she leaves home in what many would call a vain pursuit of self-knowledge. But her children can take care of themselves—nobody wears diapers anymore. The situation may not be ideal, but it's not disastrous. And we have to revere Abigail's respect for self-knowledge. The great Greek philosopher Socrates considered self-knowledge the key to a life that is worth living. We should revere a mother who would go to such extremes to demonstrate its importance to herself and, indirectly, to her children as well.

Abigail's self-sufficient spirit and pursuit of authenticity in life appear to be in short supply in the Pennsylvania suburbs, making her brave declaration of independence even more valuable. While others waste their lives in delusions, it's better for children to have a mother like Abigail show them the way of truth. Ruana Singh, for example, realizes only late in the novel that her husband has failed her and that she doesn't love him. Had Mrs. Singh been gifted with Abigail's self-understanding, she could've saved herself earlier.

We can't call either Jack or Abigail perfect. But considering the unfathomable losses they suffer, they remain true to themselves with an impressive tenacity, from the beginning of their hardships to the end.

○　○　○

# Is Sebold a religious writer?

## "YES. SEBOLD FILLS *THE LOVELY BONES* WITH RELIGIOUS ALLUSIONS AND THOUGHTS, LEAVING IT WITH A STRONG SPIRITUAL DIMENSION."

Sebold shows us the frequency and depth of her religious allusions from the first sentence of the novel. When Susie introduces herself, comparing her last name to the fish, she catches the attention of all those readers of *The Lovely Bones* who ever took a college English class in which they learned that the fish symbolizes Christ. That fish symbolism becomes even stronger when Lindsey draws a fish on her nametag—trying to hide from the popular recognition of her sister's name—and a fellow conference attendant asks whether Lindsey is religious. Even characters within the novel catch the Christian allegory behind the last name Salmon.

Susie's narration of the entire novel from heaven drives home the religious meaning that flows through Sebold's message: the storyteller literally dictates the story from the afterlife. Susie addresses us directly, as a preacher addresses his congregation, closing the novel with a warm wish that we all live long and happy lives—as if she were leaving the pulpit right when we close the book. Few novelists speak to the reader in the second person, but most church sermons do—and we feel the religious power of this form of address.

Susie has a spiritual message for us. She speaks about love and mortality, arguing that while we may feel intensely the urge to grieve those loved ones who die, and may grieve them in a long and difficult process, in the end we have to let them go. Susie learns this lesson herself and shares it with us at the conclusion of the novel, when she says she can finally withdraw from earthly affairs and content herself with heaven. She says goodbye to life, finally accepting her own death, just as the Salmons accept hers. Susie delivers an ancient truth—that all things in the mortal world must die and disappear.

Susie also delivers a strong Christian message about justice. While the human world abounds in injustices, the New Testament dictates that the wronged party must turn the other cheek, dismiss the urge to seek revenge, and leave the execution of justice to the powers of heaven. "Vengeance is mine, I shall repay," says God in the Bible: *God* will avenge, not us. Susie's tale illustrates this Christian view of vengeance by showing us the huge error of Jack Salmon's attempt at revenge. In taking divine retribution on his own shoulders, he nearly makes the unforgivable mistake of killing the wrong party. If Jack would simply leave justice to the heavenly powers, he could trust that George Harvey would eventually be punished—as we see later, when the heavenly Susie causes an icicle to fall on him and kill him.

Finally, Susie's story sends out a strong message about love and humility. From Susie's heavenly perspective, no other human attainments matter as much as caring for loved ones. Susie does value other achievements, such as education (in Lindsey) and a sense of fun and glamour (in Grandma Lynn). But when push comes to shove, what Susie values most is her father's ability to remain constant in his love for his children through hardship and pain. Jack's love keeps the family together. His ability to swallow his pride and accept Abigail with open arms when she returns shows that love, for Jack, matters more than ego or vanity. Jack's caring nature expresses the Christian ideal of love and shows how the Salmons would be lost without it.

## "NO, WE CAN'T CALL THE LOVELY BONES A RELIGIOUS NOVEL. SEBOLD'S SCATTERED REFERENCES TO RELIGION MAKE US THINK ABOUT SPIRITUALITY AND LIFE'S MEANING, BUT NOT IN THE ESTABLISHED SENSE OF RELIGION."

Sebold may label Susie's post-life place of residence as "heaven," but that place has almost nothing to do with religious conceptions of heaven in any faith. In Susie's heaven, girls read Seventeen, sit on swings, play with their dogs, and smell their favorite smells. But the Christian conception of heaven means more than a sweet-smelling playground. Heaven in the true Christian sense is a place dominated by the sanctity of God, who reigns and shines pure light over everything.

Susie never makes any mention of God, seemingly unaware of the notion of God. This omission does a lot to disqualify The Lovely Bones as a religious book. A novel set in heaven without God may make us think about the meaning of life, but it doesn't make us contemplate the truths of religion. Susie lacks any sense of a wisdom greater than her own.

Although Susie does listen to the advice of her celestial counselor, Franny, she wanders through heaven guided only by her own whims and inclinations. She seems oblivious of the Christian conception of heaven as the place of God's will. Susie has only her own will to follow.

Susie's momentary resurrection scene has almost no religious aspect to it. It may remind us of horror films or voodoo, but not at all of any major religious doctrine. According to Christianity, we alone possess our bodies even after death, when we will need them for resurrection on Judgment Day. Under Christian teaching, the dead can't inhabit the bodies of others as Susie takes up Ruth's. In the Hindu religion, on the other hand, souls may migrate to other bodies. But even in Hinduism, such reincarnation occurs at birth, not whenever a fourteen-year-old soul slips into the body of a newly dead friend. Susie's temporary takeover of Ruth is bizarre by any standard.

And most important, Susie displays a deeply unreligious motive for returning to Earth. She has been preoccupied for a long time about the grief and lost bearings of many of her family members, but concern for their welfare isn't what prompts her return. Nor does she come back to avenge evil by killing off her own murderer. Rather, Susie returns to Earth to have sex with her former school crush. She may be acting honestly and believably—and the notion of such a reason for resurrection may make us grin—but Susie doesn't show any religious consciousness at all in coming back for sexual reasons.

While Sebold gives us lots of things to think about in *The Lovely Bones* and offers us much philosophical food for thought, she gives us no real religious doctrines or ideas to mull over. As much as her novel entertains and instructs us, it doesn't embrace any specific religious outlook— or even grapple religious concerns of any kind. In the end, we really can't call it a religious novel.

○   ○   ○

# Is Sebold's portrayal of heaven traditional?

## "YES, IN MOST RESPECTS SUSIE'S HEAVEN IS QUITE TRADITIONAL."

In heaven, according to *The Lovely Bones*, happiness prevails. Wishes come true, whims are satisfied instantly, and people run from one blissful experience to the next. And we sense that people in Sebold's heaven live in such bliss—not just Susie but her grandfather, her counselor Franny, and so on—because their souls have grown light and free, finally released from their burdensome earthly existences. In this sense, Sebold's view of heaven conforms to the Christian idea of heaven passed on for millennia through art and literature. In Christian tradition, humans leave behind their lower selves on Earth as they ascend to heaven, where their purified souls are freed from strife and anxiety, and they feel only bliss.

Susie has no sex in heaven—another detail that accords with Christian convention. Although the earthly Susie sits poised on the brink of sexual experimentation after her kiss with Ray, and although she continues to feel an intense physical interest in Ray from the other world, she shows no desire to make sexual activity into part of her celestial routine. In heaven, she spends her time in art class or swinging on the swings in the school playground, not making out with boys. No one else in heaven seems bent on sex either—on the whole, Sebold's heaven strikes us as a remarkably chaste place.

In the same way, traditional Christian conceptions of heaven place virtually no emphasis on sex in the afterlife. In the Christian doctrine of St. Augustine that's been passed down through the centuries, angels have no gender at all. Naturally, angels have no need to procreate, so they feel no sexual impulses. In traditional Christian lore, sex belongs to our earthly selves rather than our purer souls: sex comes from our physical sides, not our spiritual sides.

Sebold also employs the traditional idea of heaven as a meeting place for loved ones after death. The pleasure of reunion offsets the agony of death. For Susie, heaven is like a wonderful family reunion. She can once again place her feet on her grandfather's shoes and dance to Barber's *Adagio* with him. She can once again frolic with Holiday. She knows that someday soon Grandma Lynn will stroll over and say hi.

She can even meet up with other girls her age, including some who were also victims of George Harvey. As Susie enjoys the social aspects of heaven, she reinforces the traditional Christian idea that heaven reunites separated souls.

## "NO, SUSIE'S HEAVEN IS VERY UNUSUAL—IN SOME WAYS, TOTALLY UNPRECEDENTED."

Sebold's heaven may be a believable and complete vision, but it hardly follows any traditional models. Her heavenly narrator, Susie, makes no mention whatsoever of angels—those creatures we normally associate with the Christian celestial realm. We don't know whether Susie can be called an angel now—she never refers to having wings. We don't hear about St. Peter guarding the entrance to heaven, or about the Pearly Gates. Most important, we hear nothing about God reigning over heaven. Susie makes absolutely no mention of a divine presence in the other world, or of any sense of the sacred. A heaven without God qualifies as a fascinating innovation, but we can't call it traditional.

Susie's dissatisfaction in heaven also breaks with tradition. While the traditional Christian idea of heaven involves absolute inward satisfaction and delight for its inhabitants, Susie doesn't seem blissfully happy in this heaven. On the contrary, as we watch Susie's daily activities and moods in the afterlife, we notice how unfulfilled she seems. Yes, she goes through the motions of playing with her dog after he shows up, or watching her friend spin around joyfully in circles as her dress flies up, or chatting at the swing set with her roommate. But Susie is never ecstatic in any of these activities—she's never even fully entertained. Her narration of heavenly pleasures strikes us as being even a bit bored, or at least distracted.

In similarly un-heavenly fashion, Susie focuses on Earth, not on the world of the afterlife. If she seems distracted as she swings aimlessly in the playground or appears less than constantly thrilled by the beauty magazines she flips through, we know where her mind has wandered: to her family and friends on Earth. Indeed, Susie feels these Earth yearnings so powerfully that her counselor, Franny, gently chastises her for her fixation on the life she left behind. Franny tells Susie that she must eventually let go of Earth—which seems like sensible advice, as anyone in the afterlife has by definition left their first life far behind.

But we see clearly in Susie's narrative that she can't let go of Earth. Sebold structures her whole novel around Susie's fascination with the everyday details of earthly lives, past and present—so *The Lovely Bones* itself wouldn't exist if Susie followed Franny's advice and let go of Earth. In short, Sebold's rejection of the traditional notion of heaven—that residents of heaven focus mainly on the paradise they inhabit—makes her novel possible.

While the idea of a heaven-dweller nostalgic for Earth goes against the grain of Christian doctrine, some writers and artists before Sebold have toyed with angels who miss Earth in similar fashion. The German filmmaker Wim Wenders made a moving film, known in English as *Wings of Desire* (remade as *City of Angels* with Nicolas Cage and Meg Ryan) that depicts a host of angels who spend their days longingly staying alongside Earth-dwellers as they go through their daily routines. Those angels want nothing more than simply to *live* again, possessed by the same lingering fascination with the life they left behind that grips Susie. But Wenders's angels reside on Earth and participate invisibly in earthly activities, whereas Susie unmistakably resides far away in heaven. We would expect the huge distance from her home to lessen her interest in it, but it doesn't.

Sebold fashions her particular vision of heaven not to conform to religious or literary rules, but to make it work for her novel. The place that Susie flies off to at the very end of the novel, after she's learned to let go of Earth, may well be more like a conventional Christian heaven. But the heaven we see in *The Lovely Bones* flouts traditions right and left, and has almost nothing to do with the afterlife we know from our own cultural and religious sources.

○　○　○

# What is Grandma Lynn's function in *The Lovely Bones?*

## "SEBOLD BRINGS IN GRANDMA LYNN FOR COMIC RELIEF. THE NOVEL WOULD BE TOO GLOOMY WITHOUT HER TOUCH OF OFFBEAT HUMOR."

Sebold faces the challenge every writer faces in writing about death: how to sustain our interest with page after page of grief, loss, and emotional pain. When the victim is a lively and happy fourteen-year-old girl who suffers a particularly brutal death, the challenge becomes even tougher. And when we find that the rest of the novel focuses on the emotional agony and slow disintegration that girl's death brings upon her family, we wonder how Sebold imagined she could ever write anything other than a truly dark, depressing novel.

Grandma Lynn steps into this gloomy narrative to save the day with her wit and high spirits. Appearing about halfway through the novel, Grandma Lynn arrives to care for her daughter's grieving and fragile family. She does offer some support but strikes us mainly with her straight-from-the-hip way of speaking. She peppers her talk with colorful words like "*capisce?*" in a way that no one else in the family does. She firmly believes that one should not face life without a good stiff cocktail, so she continually runs to the kitchen to fix herself a fresh highball. Grandma Lynn brings fun to the Salmon household, a scarce commodity in the aftermath of a murder.

Part of Grandma Lynn's charm lies in her blithe refusal to care for others. In a novel in which so many people try so hard to make each other feel better, this vain old lady's self-absorbed focus on her own pleasure is a refreshing bit of humor. Heaven to her doesn't mean a loving reunion with her husband or parents—it means cocktails with Dean Martin. With clear delight, Grandma Lynn wears furs and rents limousines. Though the furs are second-hand, she doesn't care what anyone might say. Inappropriate comments fly easily out of her mouth. When Buck practices the drums, she must bite her lip to keep from mentioning that most of the jazz greats drank heavily—as if only barely aware that a parent figure shouldn't say such things to a youngster.

In the Salmon family, Sebold creates such an earnest and intensely (sometimes annoyingly) well-meaning set of people that she pretty much *had* to invent Grandma Lynn for the sake of balance. Like the clowns that appear in Shakespeare's darkest tragedies, Grandma Lynn provides the drama of *The Lovely Bones* with a little spicy humor to offset its bleak introspection.

## "GRANDMA LYNN IS AN ADMIRABLE EXAMPLE OF STRENGTH AND LIFE WISDOM. SHE'S NOT JUST COMIC RELIEF—SHE REPRESENTS A HUMAN IDEAL THAT SEBOLD TAKES SERIOUSLY."

Sebold associates Grandma Lynn with a free sexuality that the Salmon parents lack, and that blows through the novel like a refreshing breeze. She flirts with any man in sight, sometimes even her son-in-law. Still thin and shapely at about seventy, Grandma Lynn cares for herself and her appearance. This older woman may display what seem like superficial virtues in eating right and looking good, but they may be important ones to teenage girls.

Grandma Lynn's comfort with sex reminds both Salmon girls that sex should be fun, not associated with pain or degradation. Love and violence frequently connect in the Salmons' world, as in Shakespeare's *Othello*, which Susie reads in school. After Susie's brutal rape, we have trouble imagining Lindsey growing up to lead a healthy sexual life. She may always fear that a first kiss—like Susie's kiss with Ray—will lead to some mortal punishment. In such a charged atmosphere, Grandma soothes everyone with her constant message about the acceptability of sex. She discusses issues of puberty straightforwardly. She encourages Lindsey to start shaving her legs, while Jack awkwardly asserts that Lindsey is too young.

This solid older woman provides strength to the Salmon family in a way no one else can. She may drink too much and spend too much money, but she remains there for the family in an indispensable way. She represents goodwill and caring without the stodginess of conservative family values. With her slinky clothes and cocktails, she wants everyone to have fun and treat each other well. The notion of holding a family together at all costs would mean little to Grandma Lynn, but she does love her own family.

Grandma Lynn has her own views but never lectures or judges—an important lesson in a novel about forgiveness. While she dislikes Abigail's affair, she doesn't say so directly but simply points out that Abigail's father had carried on an affair for years. In a way, Grandma Lynn gives Abigail backhanded permission to pursue her fling when she sends out the message that adultery may be forgiven as time goes by. We can't call this advice incorrect, as Jack eventually does forgive Abigail, and their marriage may in fact deepen as a result. In this sense, Grandma may preside like a wise old owl over the most radical move Abigail ever makes in her life.

Sebold gives Grandma Lynn due credit by having Susie comment that, to her own surprise, her grandma matters to her more than any other family member. With all the love Susie shows her brother, sister, and parents throughout the novel, this statement comes as extremely high praise. But Susie means every word of it. Grandma Lynn shows a commitment to life in all its merry vitality that Susie, deprived of life, can finally appreciate. Grandma Lynn proves herself independent and resourceful but devoted to her family, showing just the right balance between self and family that the other characters strive—not always successfully—to achieve.

○   ○   ○

## Does Susie and Ruth's bodily swap indicate some deep soul connection between the two girls or is it just a coincidence?

### "RUTH AND SUSIE ARE TOTALLY DIFFERENT CHARACTERS WITH DISSIMILAR PERSONALITIES. THE CONTACT IS JUST A COINCIDENCE AND HAS NO DEEP MEANING IN THE NOVEL."

The contact between Ruth and Susie occurs entirely by chance, because Susie happens to be in the right place at the right time. She loves to follow Ray on his daily activities, and Ray happens to accompany Ruth on the day of Ruth's near-death experience. Susie takes over

Ruth's body because that body is conveniently located near Ray. The proximity between the two girls has a lot to do with their common affections for Ray but little to do with anything they share between the two of them.

The best proof that Susie doesn't relate deeply to Ruth lies in Susie's total focus on Ray after her return to Earth, her almost complete disregard for the soul of the girl whose body she now occupies. After her resurrection, Susie fixates on Ray. All her actions focus on him: she looks into his eyes, she guesses what he thinks, she takes a shower with him, and she has sex with him. Throughout this experience, Susie uses Ruth's body but hardly spares a moment to speculate on what Ruth experiences on her way to heaven, whether the celestial authorities will tell her she will return to Earth, and so on. Susie doesn't cruelly ignore Ruth, but her total absorption in Ray at Ruth's expense does lead us to believe that there's no deep connection between the two girls, no underlying reason for their brief crossover.

## "SUSIE AND RUTH SHARE A LOT, FROM THEIR INDEPENDENCE OF SPIRIT AND EMOTIONAL HONESTY TO THEIR AFFECTION FOR RAY. THE CONTACT BETWEEN THE TWO GIRLS SYMBOLIZES EVERYTHING THEY SHARE. "

Though Susie had only minimal contact with Ruth while alive, Ruth's development after Susie's death brings out key similarities between the personalities of the two girls. Susie grasps these similarities as she watches Ruth from heaven. Susie views Ruth as living out the freethinking, free-living side of Susie's own self that would have emerged had Susie survived. Susie's brush with Ruth on the path between Earth and heaven symbolizes the deep connection the two girls share. It shows how in both body and soul they have made a lasting contact, despite the distance between death and life.

Susie's death affects Ruth almost as deeply as it affects Lindsey and the other members of the Salmon family, even though Ruth never seems to have been a close friend of Susie during her lifetime. But in death Susie becomes a profound influence on Ruth. Ruth starts writing poetry— poetry that we gather has a feminist slant to it. Ruth may be the only one in the novel to think politically and culturally about Susie's rape and what it reflects about the relations between men and women. The connection between Susie and Ruth marks the dawning of a political awareness in Ruth. Susie's contact with Ruth when Susie returns to Earth symbolizes the intellectual influence between the two.

The brush between Susie and Ruth also serves as an emblem of the independent spirit the two girls share. Susie's motto in her junior-high yearbook instructs us to write against the lines on ruled paper, following our own direction in everything we do. This phrase could be the motto by which Ruth lives her later life, when she braves poverty and abjection in moving to a closet on the Lower East Side of New York City. While Ruth in her black, bohemian garb couldn't come across as less like the young Susie in her pom-pom hat and mittens back in 1973, still both exhibit a feistiness and curiosity about life that sets them apart from their peers. We feel that had Susie lived, she might well have ended up as Ruth's roommate in New York City. The contact between the two reminds us of how the two girls' personalities mirror one another.

○   ○   ○

In crime tales, we usually yearn to see the criminals captured. Why does Sebold not choose to have George Harvey finally caught by the police?

**"SEBOLD HAS NO REASON TO SHOW HARVEY GETTING CAUGHT. IT WOULDN'T CHANGE ANY-THING, SINCE THE DAMAGE HAS ALREADY BEEN DONE AND WE KNOW THE MURDERER'S IDENTITY."**

Sebold has explained in interviews that in reading about murder cases she tends to be drawn to the victim's point of view rather than the murderer's. She claims that most crime novels and non-fiction works about crime tend to focus on the perpetrator's identity, thoughts, and feelings. We might agree. Bookstores offer us several full-length studies of Ted

Bundy, for example, but not a single full-length book about any of the women he killed. In *The Lovely Bones*, Sebold chooses to focus on someone other than Harvey.

Sebold might have felt poetic justice in showing Harvey apprehended by the police in a different sort of novel, one that focused less centrally on Susie and her family. If Sebold had written a fictional biography of Harvey the serial killer, we would demand to see more of the police investigation and the attempts to trace Harvey's escape from town. We would be more interested in exploring Harvey's twisted mind and deranged motivation for killing girls. We might want to find out how he managed to own a home in Susie's neighborhood without leaving a paper trail behind him. If the novel were about Harvey, then we would yearn for a scene of capture and arrest. We would demand that a book about a successful killer justify itself by bringing justice down on him in the end.

But *The Lovely Bones* focuses on Susie, not Harvey or the idea of serial murder. After Susie dies, it hardly matters what happens to Harvey. Susie's demise becomes the motivating force of the novel's plot and its emotional anchor. A scene of Harvey's final arrest might detract from Susie's central role, as our attention would shift away from her martyred self in heaven toward earthly institutions of justice that define Susie as a police case and a crime casualty. If Sebold had shined the spotlight too much on Harvey, she would've risked focusing on earthly matters too much and turning Susie into a statistic.

## "IF SEBOLD SHOWED HARVEY'S ARREST, SHE'D SEND A MESSAGE THAT GOOD TRIUMPHS OVER EVIL IN THE WORLD. BUT SHE WANTS TO MAKE THE OPPOSITE POINT ABOUT LIFE ON EARTH— THAT EVIL GOES ON AND ON."

While Harvey's arrest would certainly have given us a rousing, optimistic ending to *The Lovely Bones*, Sebold didn't aim to write an optimistic novel—she aimed to write a realistic one. She wished to strip us of the rose-colored lenses we often wear, to show us that happy endings may conclude drugstore novels but don't always come through in real life. Good does exist in the world, but evil does too. Life consists of a constant tug-of-war between the two, with no winner ever declared. If Sebold had shown

Harvey captured after killing Susie, she'd be guilty of oversimplifying the moral map of the world she paints for us. She prefers instead to say that life doesn't always illustrate the triumph of good.

George Harvey becomes a symbol of an important, though unlikable, aspect of our moral reality—evil. In that regard, he becomes indispensable to the novel. Sebold finds it necessary to keep Harvey on the loose for the same reason that Christianity finds it necessary to keep Satan lurking behind the scenes of human activities. Both these figures of evil contaminate the world with their wickedness and symbolize the pain, grief, and suffering that life contains. The continuing existence of George Harvey, like the existence of the devil, reminds us of our fallen status, of the inevitable imperfections and failings of the world in which we live.

But we shouldn't conclude that Sebold means to write an ultimately pessimistic novel. On the contrary, she wishes to drive home the wickedness of the world in order to emphasize the forgiveness, patience, and saolidarity we need to dwell in it each day. She sends out the lesson loud and clear in *The Lovely Bones*: we desperately need to stick together, because bad things happen all around us. Evil robs us of what we love, and in order to fill the vacuum left behind, we must take care to forge sufficient human connections, to build protective structures of human relationships—the structure of relationships that Susie refers to as "the lovely bones." Sebold names the novel after the connections that form between human beings to offset evil.

Indirectly, evil in the world gives meaning to the idea of good. Blessings would mean less to us without the evils of the world to contrast with them. In the Middle Ages, scholars regularly defended the necessity of Satan in precisely this way—the very existence of evil gave good its significance and function. Sebold demonstrates the same notion in *The Lovely Bones*. The freely wandering George Harvey—who continues to perpetrate his evil acts, as Susie informs us about his next victim—shows us human cruelty and sin. But by contrast he makes us (and the Salmon family) more aware than ever before of the crucial importance of human love, affection, and tenderness.

# A Bolt from the Blue

After years of failure and frustration as a writer, Sebold suddenly reached the height of literary fame with *The Lovely Bones*.

○   ○   ○

WHILE *THE LOVELY BONES* MAY SEEM the product of an experienced novelist, it comes to us as Alice Sebold's first novel—one published after many years of failure. Prior to this breakout novel, Sebold wrote two and a half manuscripts that didn't sell. She's said in an interview that she failed for so long that she felt her hopes for commercial success had all but vanished.

The realistic atmosphere of grief in the Salmon household in *The Lovely Bones* has a great deal to do with all the personal grieving Sebold has gone through. Loss became a way of life for her in New York City in the 1980s, when several of her friends died of AIDS. But she also underwent a bit of her own hell which influenced the novel in an even more direct way—an agony reminiscent of Susie's horrendous experience just before death. As a freshman at Syracuse University, Sebold was raped in a nearby tunnel, an enclosed, outdoor space that reminds us of George Harvey's bunker in *The Lovely Bones*.

After her assault, Sebold suffered from an extreme form of post-traumatic stress disorder but managed to keep her distinctive wit alive throughout the ordeal. The morning after her rape, Sebold's father asked her whether she would like something to eat. Sebold replied that she would, since the only things she had had in her mouth in the last twenty-four hours were a cracker and a penis. We hear this somewhat startling, straightforward, no-nonsense voice in Susie's narration throughout *The Lovely Bones*.

## The Lovely Bones

The aftermath of the rape extended the painful ordeal for Sebold, who suffered through the court trial of her assailant. Sebold's determination to survive the pain gave her strength and a new perspective on life, and we can feel her attempts to carry on with life well-illustrated in the Salmon family's struggle to get by after losing Susie. Sebold documented her feelings and experiences in *Lucky*, an acclaimed memoir of her rape and its consequences published in 1999, three years before *The Lovely Bones* appeared. In some ways, we can see the novel reworking and carrying to a higher level Sebold's insights of her more documentary memoir.

While we can never know for sure the links between biography and fiction in a writer's work, Sebold in interviews has mentioned her affinity with the victims of crime—a psychological connection that we imagine has something to do with her own survival of sexual assault. She has said that she has read so many stories over the years that focus on the experience and mindset of murderers that her interest in the victim's point of view grew stronger. This focus on the victim's perspective became a defining and distinctive trait of *The Lovely Bones*.

Born in 1963, Alice Sebold grew up in the suburbs of Philadelphia not far from where Susie Salmon lives and dies in the novel. Her mother worked as a newspaper journalist in the area, which may have given Sebold the interest in news bulletins she later describes as prompting her literary development. As a girl, Sebold used to make up stories for the pictures of dead girls she saw in the newspapers. Sebold's father was a professor of Spanish, a career mirroring that of Ray Singh's father in *The Lovely Bones*. (Mr. Singh teaches postcolonial history at Penn, and his wife takes a dim view of his profession.)

### Love is blind

Sebold met her husband, the novelist Glen David Gold, on her first day in California, when he arrived on campus on a motorcycle and couldn't remove his helmet. Gold is best known as the author of a novel about vaudeville magicians in early twentieth-century America, *Carter Beats the Devil*, which was based on historical research of the period. Like his wife, Gold wrote several novels that went unpublished before hitting the goldmine with *Carter*.

In religious terms, Sebold had a relaxed upbringing. Her family practiced what Sebold described in an interview as a "wishy-washy Episcopalian" faith that gave her an awareness of the basic facts of heaven and salvation, but in a vague and imprecise way. She reports that she used to read comic books in the pew, in somewhat the same way that Susie reads *Vogue* and *Seventeen* in heaven. Interestingly, some religiously devout readers of *The Lovely Bones* make similar critical objections to the portrayal of heaven in the novel, which they find incomprehensibly devoid of God and Jesus.

After college, Sebold taught freshman composition writing in New York City for ten years, also working as a research analyst. She lived in the bohemian East Village, not far from where her character Ruth ends up sleeping in a closet. Sebold experimented with heroin for two years. Then, with a student loan, she left New York for California, where she enrolled in a creative writing program. On her first day of orientation at UC Irvine, she met a man who arrived late and couldn't manage to get his motorcycle helmet off—a man named Glen David Gold, a writer himself who would eventually become Sebold's husband. Sebold and Gold live in California to this day.

Sebold describes herself as a character-focused writer. More important even than the right plot, a good set of characters makes a successful novel. In interviews she speaks of the importance of listening carefully to one's characters, treating them as living people with their own spheres of experience that we can plug into if we listen hard enough. But Sebold doesn't neglect the importance of style, as many reviewers noted when they praised *The Lovely Bones* for its unexpected lyrical beauty. Sebold notes that she often uses poets—two of her favorites are James Tate and Elizabeth Bishop—as springboards for reaching the right language and cadence in her prose.

In terms of literary influence from other writers, Sebold has declared the American novelist Henry James to be her literary hero. Some may find this strange, since James's convoluted sentence structure and highly abstract language contrast sharply with the matter-of-fact straightforwardness of Sebold's prose. But in choice of theme we can see a similarity between the two writers. Several of James's best known novels and stories focus on naïve American girls, like Isabel Archer in *Portrait of a Lady* or the teenaged Daisy in *Daisy Miller*, who face an experience that forces them to confront guilt and sin in the world. Sebold makes this same theme of the end of innocence her primary concern in *The Lovely Bones*.

# Behind the Picket Fence

Susie's tragedy takes place in a suburban dreamland that—much like America itself at the time—isn't as familiar as it seems.

○  ○  ○

SEBOLD PRESENTS THE SALMONS' Pennsylvania suburb as a kind of idyllic throwback to a rosy national past, a little patch of 1950s optimism alive and well in the early 1970s. The Salmons' residential neighborhood provides such a cushy nest of security and safety that no one in it seems to view crime as a real possibility—as we see in the police department's amateurish and clumsy attempts to investigate a murder, perhaps the first in their precinct. Susie tells us that no one sees George Harvey when he takes her dismembered body off to the sinkhole on some industrial outskirts of town, because in those days a night watchman wasn't considered a necessity. People trust each other in this town. Neighbors know each other and speak to one another, never suspecting until too late that one of them may be a psychopath.

But just as the neighborhood harbors the unseen evil of George Harvey behind one of its picket fences, so too does the America we see in *The Lovely Bones* contain the seeds of its later social problems. The year 1973 found the country deeply divided. Part of the nation clung to the post-World War II belief in American excellence and world leadership and believed that U.S. military and economic power could do no wrong. But another part—by 1973 a growing segment of the population under the age of thirty—vehemently opposed American military involvement in Vietnam, which they considered an imperialistic campaign. Many of the older generation of Americans at the time never even conceived of doubting or criticizing the policies of their own government, and an acrimonious national debate about American values ensued. In *The Lovely Bones*, we don't hear much discussion of Vietnam in the Salmon family. But Sebold subtly reminds us of the folly of male violence as a solution to problems when Jack's raging foray into the cornfield to nab the murderer turns out to be an error of judgment that nearly takes innocent lives.

Other Americans also began to wonder to what extent the American state really represented their interests and began to demand that their voices be heard. The Singh family (though from India rather than Vietnam) surely asks questions about what it means to be American, being the only dark-skinned family in Fairfax. Gay men and women started to become more open about their sexuality, seeking a place at the American table like everyone else. We don't hear much about homosexuality in *The Lovely Bones*, but it does come up once when Ray tells Ruth he had assumed she liked girls. When Ruth candidly replies that she could fool around with Ray by pretending that he was Susie, she reveals her lesbian interests with an ease that would've been unthinkable even ten years earlier.

In the 1970s, women sought to express themselves in new, unprecedented ways. Feminist writers like Doris Lessing, Betty Friedan, and Gloria Steinem inspired a whole generation of young women to rethink the traditional wisdom that forced women into the kitchen and bedroom as wives and mothers. Abigail says she wishes Gloria Steinem would trim her fingernails, but she also feels mildly ashamed to say so—admitting her basic respect for the feminist writer. Institutions of higher education

## Stranger than fiction

One day when Sebold was growing up in suburbs much like those where the Salmon family lives, she and her family were watching television when a neighborhood couple was hit by a car and thrown wounded into the Sebolds' front lawn. The man who hit the couple stopped long enough to tell two boys playing basketball that the couple needed an ambulance—and then proceeded to drive three houses down the street where he lived and walked calmly into his home. Sebold uses this anecdote to illustrate how the suburbs can provide the novelist with far odder material than anything found in New York City—a setting she tried to base a novel on before returning to a suburban locale in *The Lovely Bones.*

had admitted women almost universally by 1970, and girls were expected to attend college just like their brothers. We hear that the highly educated Abigail Salmon, who reads French novels for fun, had to fight tooth and nail with Grandma Lynn for her right to higher schooling. But by Lindsey's generation, girls don't have to fight anymore to get the highest possible education, even in math and science, where Lindsey excels.

Beyond the need for equal education, 1970s-era feminism also taught women the need for self-examination and self-discovery, that women shouldn't follow the orders of others but should seek out meaning in their own lives, on their own terms. Abigail carries out this injunction in an extreme fashion when she cheats on her husband, leaves her family, and goes to California to work at a winery—northern California was a center of liberal and feminist values. Abigail doesn't feel the need to provide any justification for going—to her family or to herself—other than as a chance to find herself. In similar fashion, Ruth's quirky pursuit of her dreams in New York City shows a disdain for living by anyone's rules other than her own.

As both women and men began to pursue their individual aims more than ever, the nuclear family began to lose its traditional shape and cohesion. Divorce rates skyrocketed in the 1970s, and single-parent families—like the Salmon household, run by Jack and his mother-in-law Lynn—began to spread. Marriage lost its earlier sanctity, as we see symbolized in the flirtations between Len Fenerman and Abigail Salmon, and between Jack Salmon and Ruana Singh. Within the family, generational conflicts arose. Parents no longer found their words revered like scripture but viewed with skepticism, as many young Americans declared they would never trust anyone over age thirty. The fourteen-year-old Lindsey takes on the thirty-six-year-old George Harvey and wins.

Similarly, American attitudes toward sex loosened considerably in the 1970s. While sex before marriage would've been a serious taboo in Grandma Lynn's day, by the time Lindsey reaches adolescence it's become acceptable, perhaps even expected. Attending a symposium with Samuel, Lindsey feels no shame in reaching over and initiating sex with him in a bold way. They have sex long before the question of marriage ever arises. Ray and Ruth casually accept that they fool around with each other without any pretense of romance on either side.

## The Lovely Bones

In the broadest sense, America in the 1970s displayed a dynamism and capacity for social and cultural change that we feel throughout *The Lovely Bones*. The landscape changes as suburbs spread into what were cornfields only years earlier; society changes as people find new priorities for their lives and rethink the old institutions of marriage and family life. Most important, the Salmon family changes as they come to grips with the loss of Susie and with the evolving nation around them.

# A Well-Timed Tale

*The Lovely Bones* launched into bookstores at a time when America was particularly primed for Sebold's story and message.

○   ○   ○

WHEN THE LOVELY BONES APPEARED in bookshelves in the summer of 2002, it found the United States in a frame of mind perfectly suited for Sebold's message. Not only did Sebold's theme of the end of American suburban innocence find a deep resonance in the nation's gloomy worries in the aftermath of the September 11 tragedy, but the climate of anxiety about the sexual abuse of children in America had also reached a fever pitch. The Catholic church faced unprecedented numbers of lawsuits accusing priests of unlawful sexual manipulation of minors, and the similarity to George Harvey's seduction and rape of Susie Salmon was too close for comfort. Moreover, the summer of 2002 coincidentally saw the spread of popular concern — even hysteria — about the kidnappings of several young girls across the U.S. Eerily, this list of missing girls included a Utah girl named Elizabeth Smart, who disappeared at the same age that Susie did — fourteen — and shared Susie's vibrant personality and friendly demeanor. More than a few reviewers in 2002 made mention of Elizabeth Smart in their articles on *The Lovely Bones.* (Miraculously, Elizabeth Smart was found alive nine months after her abduction, in March 2003.)

Many early reviewers expressed surprise that the novel's gimmicky premise actually followed through with some highly sophisticated writing and philosophical depth. Laura Miller, writing in *Salon,* expected sentimentality from a story of a raped and murdered fourteen-year-old girl but found to her amazement that Sebold's style "wards off mawkishness like a voodoo charm." Similarly, Connie Ogle, writing in the *Houston Chronicle*, acknowledged that the concept of *The Lovely Bones* "may sound vaguely precious" but assured potential readers that it wasn't. *January* magazine's Tony Buchsbaum found it gratifying to discover an example of a crowd-pleasing gimmick—like a girl narrating her own murder from heaven—that an author could then carry through impressively.

Some writers commented that *The Lovely Bones*, with its impressive verbal artistry, would reach a more educated audience than a less polished novel would have. Acknowledging the power of Sebold's tough and serious style, Miller predicted that *The Lovely Bones* would attract and touch a more highbrow audience than its sentimental-sounding subject matter would at first indicate.

In the same vein, the influential *New York Times* reviewer Michiko Kakutani admitted that she had vague expectations that *The Lovely Bones* would aim for cheap, heart-tugging effects along the lines of the 1990 blockbuster movie *Ghost*. But Sebold's novel ultimately surprised Kakutani with its complex rendering of family dynamics and its precise annotation of the "mathematics of love" existing between parents and children. Miller found gentleness in Sebold's novel but saw it as genuine rather than cheap and sentimental. She compared the experience of reading *The Lovely Bones* to being "wrapped in a warm blanket after a trauma." Miller felt that Sebold achieved the feel-good effects of maudlin fiction but made those effects real and affecting.

Many critics praised Sebold for avoiding the sensationalistic, grandiose aspects of Susie's death and focusing instead on the Salmon family's

## Kindred spirits

In a review of *The Lovely Bones,* the popular writer Anna Quindlen favorably compared Sebold's novel to Harper Lee's 1960 bestseller, *To Kill a Mockingbird.* Coincidentally, Lee's novel appears in Sebold's—on Susie's English class reading list. It turns out that Sebold and Lee have a few notable things in common: both were from small-town backgrounds, both spent time in New York City, and both burst quickly into public fame with their best-selling first published novels narrated by young girls, both of which novels revolve around a violent action committed by a social outcast.

humdrum daily attempts to keep its sanity in the face of disaster. Kaku-tani lauded Sebold's knack for capturing "both the ordinary and the extraordinary." Buchsbaum compared the everyday familiarity we have with the Salmon family by the end of *The Lovely Bones* to the author's creation of a kind of "narrated photo album," as if we've been sitting with an acquaintance who has told us her life story over several hours. These critics also applauded Sebold for refusing to overdramatize Susie's poten-tially melodramatic tale, and for keeping a more restrained voice that nevertheless always manages to hold our interest.

The balance of darkness and optimism in *The Lovely Bones* also attracted critical praise. On the one hand Susie speaks with the warm and fuzzy voice of a fourteen-year-old babe in the woods, but on the other hand we can never forget that she's been doomed to exile from the world she cares so much about. Geoff Parkes, writing in the offbeat series *Delu-sions of Adequacy Book Reviews*, loved that we're constantly aware throughout *The Lovely Bones* that the ending will never turn out happy, since the narrator has already died. Parkes saw the darkness of the novel as representing the end of innocence for a whole generation of Ameri-cans in the early 1970s—the bright optimism of the earlier part of the century was ending for good, and Susie's gloomy tale symbolizes that end. In this respect, Parkes compares Sebold's novel to Ang Lee's 1997 film *The Ice Storm*, which recounts a similar story of lost innocence in a suburban household in the early 1970s.

Many commentators noted that Sebold employs many of the devices of the whodunit or crime novel but avoids letting her novel slide into that literary genre completely. Karen Valby in *Entertainment Weekly* expressed relief that *The Lovely Bones* never degenerates into what she calls the "Aha!" style of crime investigation. She praised Sebold for bypassing the intricacies of the police investigation of Susie's case— indeed, we never hear much about Len Fenerman's progress on the case after his affair with Abigail ends—and focusing instead on the emotions and the family dynamics of the Salmon household.

Sebold also drew praise for her ability to integrate comic relief into such a bleak postmortem novel. Several reviewers found Grandma Lynn delightful, wandering through the narrative in designer clothes with a highball in her hand. Others liked the fresh and humorous adoption of a young teen perspective, as in the fact that the high school textbooks Susie uses in heaven include *Vogue*. Joy Press in *The Village Voice* enjoyed the fact that the "morbidly obsessed" Ruth fittingly wins a considerable amount of fame in the afterlife—but that her renown is just like earthly fame, "a bunch of teenagers poring over an issue of *TeenBeat*."

Many reviewers—and not just those in religious publications—noted the religious dimension of *The Lovely Bones*. Not surprisingly, some Christian readers expressed amazement—even sometimes outrage—at the fact that Susie's heaven contains no explicit presence of God or Jesus. Others accepted that Sebold aimed to be spiritual without being narrowly religious. Ron Charles in *The Christian Science Monitor* called *The Lovely Bones* "ecumenical to a fault," adding a whiff of disapproval to what sounds like general praise for Sebold's straying from Christian dogma.

# Other Books of Interest

Although Sebold breaks new ground with her novel, others before her have explored death and family from similar perspectives.

○ ○ ○

### TO KILL A MOCKINGBIRD
by Harper Lee (Lippincott, 1960)

Lee's classic story—which appears in *The Lovely Bones* as the next novel on Susie's English class reading list—tells of a social misfit named Boo Radley who terrifies the children in a small Southern town despite being childlike himself. *To Kill a Mockingbird* also features a child narrator who sounds much like Susie Salmon—largely innocent but just worldly and experienced enough to be aware of human failings and wrongdoings.

### IN COLD BLOOD
by Truman Capote (Random House, 1966)

Capote's chilling true-crime masterpiece, a pioneering work in journalistic fiction, tells the story of two vagrants who cut down an entire Kansas farm family with little compunction or guilt. Capote focuses non-judgmentally on the mindsets of the two killers in much the same way that Sebold allows us inside George Harvey's head in *The Lovely Bones*.

### WHITE NOISE
by Don DeLillo (Viking, 1985)

True, there aren't any murders in this famous novel about the fear of death in the modern American suburbs, and DeLillo's style is more underhandedly humorous than Sebold aims to be. His study of the gradual disintegration of family ties in an American household shares more than a passing similarity to Sebold's portrait of the unraveling Salmon family.

### THE FIFTH CHILD
by Doris Lessing (Knopf, 1988)
Although narrated in a tough prose style far from Sebold's gentle lyricism, Lessing's novel resembles *The Lovely Bones* in its focus on the tumult caused by one of the children in a loving family. In Lessing's case, the child is mentally ill rather than murdered, but the consequences for the family prove just as painful.

### THE AWAKENING
by Kate Chopin (1899)
Chopin's landmark feminist novel recounts a woman's sudden discovery that she feels unfulfilled by her role as wife and mother. *The Awakening* not only illuminates the character of Abigail in *The Lovely Bones*, but also gives us perspective to the attempts of the whole array of Sebold's women—including Lindsey and Grandma Lynn—to negotiate between caring for others and taking care of themselves.

### THE EXECUTIONER'S SONG
by Norman Mailer (Little, Brown, 1979)
Mailer focuses his classic study of the criminal mind on a serial killer not unlike George Harvey, though Mailer spends far less time than Sebold does on the victims. Much like Sebold, Mailer raises questions about the need for human forgiveness and love in a cruel, fallen world.

### AS I LAY DYING
by William Faulkner (Cape and Smith, 1930)
A dead old woman, matriarch of a large and unruly Southern clan, narrates Faulkner's novel in the first-person—one of the few major examples of postmortem storytelling before *The Lovely Bones*. Like Susie, Faulkner's narrator watches in semi-detached anguish the effects of her death on her family, especially on two of her sons.